AF505169

A Rose by Any Other Name

Shape Up or Shift Out Book 1

MANDY ROSKO

Copyright © 2023 by Mandy Rosko

All rights reserved.

No part of this book may be reproduced in any form or by any electronic or mechanical means, including information storage and retrieval systems, without written permission from the author, except for the use of brief quotations in a book review.

CHAPTER

ONE

Rita Procyon loved to steal other people's shit.

It was her gift and her curse.

Namely because people since time immemorial seemed to think stealing was bad. It was. But it was also fun, which she wished they could understand.

Nothing could match the thrill of it, though. Organizing a job, getting the information on the target, learning the schedules of the guards and security teams, and then outwitting them all.

Even now, her fingers twitched and itched to stroke over something expensive, something with enough girth to be heavy, but capable of being stuffed into a bag and walked off with.

Some items glittered and sparked and *screamed* at her for freedom. She was just setting them free.

Putting them out into the world.

With her.

The fact that raccoons were notorious thieves, and she was a raccoon shifter, had nothing to do with any of it.

She was pretty sure.

1

Sometimes, if the item was small enough, all Rita needed to do was shift, hide her prize away in a tree, and stick around to watch the wonderful aftermath. The stupid faces security guards made when they realized they'd had one pulled over them was the absolute best.

'How did this happen? No one could have gotten past me. I didn't see anyone come this way.'

She'd thought about investing in small cameras. Then she could replay the scenes over and over, at home, eating popcorn and praising herself for outwitting the fools who thought they were so much better than everyone else.

But, no. She'd have to keep it all recorded in her brain only because all it would take was one shit-head who knew their way around a computer, who could track her down. So her paranoia won out over the need to see her targets squirm.

Getting away was the easy part, especially if she was shifted. All she had to do was hang around the trash bins, pretend to have a snack, and she'd get shooed away. After all, no one *actually* thought a raccoon would be stealing from the rich man's house.

Raccoons were amazing. Rita thought so. She loved being a raccoon.

She was a floofy, mischievous little devil, and since no one wanted to get near her in that shape—due to their bigoted ideas of raccoons being full of diseases instead of full of awesome—it made it all the easier for her to make her escape.

She could climb trees. She could slink around roofs and garages, and no one would think twice about it. No one would suspect what was coming.

Sometimes people spotted her, and they got out the

hose to try to chase her away, but no one called the cops on her.

Not really.

Her favorite jobs were the ones on targets who deserved it, but that wasn't always the case. She couldn't always pick and choose who was going to get a visit from the amazing, masked menace in the night, but that came with the job.

If there was ever someone who *definitely* didn't deserve it—like a single mom or some struggling guy who was just trying to earn some cash for his kids—she turned the job down. Rita didn't flatter herself by thinking she was a modern female version of Robin Hood, but there was still something to be said about having honor amongst thieves. She'd rather eat Ramen for dinner for a week and pay her rent late than deal with the blight on her conscious because some dickhead wanted revenge on their ex.

"Yes, Rita, I get it. You're a great thief, but you have morals. Unfortunately, offering your services in exchange for mine just isn't how this all works." Said the woman in front of her.

Not only a shifter. More than a witch. She was... *Something*. Some*one* important.

Powerful.

And Rita needed her, but she didn't know how to prove herself.

Esme Baer was a beautiful woman, with long black hair and a good fashion sense. She was also something of a legend—meaning, her name was synonymous with matchmaking, yet no one knew how to contract her help.

The fact that Rita was sitting across from her now was nothing short of a miracle.

And possibly Rita's only chance.

Rita clenched her teeth, trying for calm.

Difficult to pull off when this whole thing was embarrassing.

"Okay, please. You don't understand. I'm not some ferocious wolf, some perfect mate for an alpha. None of the packs are interested. Pack mothers would die before letting a raccoon mate with their sons."

The woman sniffed and eyed Rita, offended. "As one who is easily underestimated, you'd do well not to underestimate others. I've matched countless shifters. I *do* understand the difficulties you face."

Rita groaned, but she did know. Even if she didn't want to admit it.

This lady had...a gift. She found people for each other. Romantically.

"Anything else, sugar?" Rita didn't so much as jump as the waitress came by.

She and Esme were the only ones in the cafe. It was almost closing time, and the older woman waitress was probably hoping for a good tip.

"You got any more Apple fritter donuts left?" Screw losing weight. Not when Rita was this stressed.

"Three, about to toss them for the night. Are you sure you want—"

"I'll take all three," Rita said. "And that last banana loaf, please. You can put them in take-out bags. We won't be long."

The waitress nodded and hurried off.

The matchmaker smiled, amused, from behind her paper tea cup. "You're not shy about eating. Perhaps a bear shifter would be suited for you."

"Don't care so long as it's a true mate."

This woman had many matches under her belt that ended in marriage, kids, the house and happiness, and all that greeting card stuff Rita had been thinking about for the last couple of years.

"Why not seek out another raccoon? I hear there are usually similar interests, and the families are tight-knit, for the most part."

A little *too* tightly knit for Rita.

She shivered.

Settling down entirely and retiring from the game wasn't in Rita's immediate sights, but she was in her thirties now. A little lonely for someone to come home to after a job well done, a meal, and a good snuggle on the couch with some nice sex after.

She still had time for a ring and kids a little later, but if she ever wanted that option, she needed to start thinking about it.

It wasn't just about finding the right *fit*. If she was going to avoid other raccoons, then she had to set up shop with her true mate. Banging random guys wouldn't satisfy Rita in the long run. She did want a happily ever after.

She wanted the real deal, and she might not have her timeline exactly set up yet, but she was working on it. That was the important thing.

"You know it's not like there are raccoon shifter families I can just pop in and find a mate in. We're not exactly common."

The witch across from Rita nodded sagely, reaching for her teacup and taking a long sip.

"Yes, I do understand that. But what I do isn't a simple dating service. I'm interested in helping you, but there's no jumping up a list of some sort, no matter what you offer me. You could offer to steal the Crown Jewels themselves, but that's not going to make your perfect mate appear. I promise the moment I have anything for you, you'll hear from me."

"I barely found you in the first place," Rita snapped.

"You didn't find me. I let you come to me."

Which was true. And if she walked out of there, Rita was terrified she would never see her again.

The woman put some money down on the table, eying Rita harshly. "Do not take this."

"I won't." Rita wouldn't steal from a waitress.

Maybe it was too much to ask for a little trust when she was a bit too proud of her profession and reputation as a thief.

The woman stood up. Rita with her.

The waitress returned. "Oh, here's your bag, would you like the check?"

"Yes, please," Rita said, not taking her eyes off the witch as the waitress walked off again.

"How will I find you again?"

The woman smiled, her soft pink lips pulling sweetly at the corners. "I'll find you, I think. Don't worry. I'll work something out."

Rita wasn't ready to let her go, but the woman didn't just walk out the door and to a car.

She vanished.

And that was that.

Rita lost her, the woman who had been impossible to find, and who only showed up because she wanted to.

For two months.

Rita had almost given up on the whole stupid idea.

Until now.

Rita's mystery matchmaking witch acquaintance had sent her a letter out of the blue.

How the hell did she know where I lived?

No one knew where Rita lived.

There wasn't even a return address, but that letter, written in a dainty, delicate script, definitely came from the witch.

I've thought about our talk, darling, and I might have something to interest you. I simply need a favor. I'm sure your services will be of use.

Rita had checked the back of the letter.

Blank.

She'd put the note under heat in case there was a hidden message.

Also nothing.

There wasn't even a stamp, return address, or phone number.

It was creepy.

But there were some instructions.

A date, address, and room number.

Excitement bubbled up inside her.

This was it. Rita knew that Esme wouldn't have just changed her mind about a barter—the creepy witch lady had a lead on Rita's mate! The time had come!

A favor. Okay. Rita could do that.

A secretive witch woman probably got by on a lot of favors.

So Rita searched the address, surprised to find it was in a residential location.

Really? Not a tall, corporate or soulless government building?

Sure, it was in a well-off neighborhood, but she'd assumed the witch would want her to infiltrate some evil corporation for secrets or something. Maybe the secret algorithm from one of the big-name matchmaking sites. Surely they kept that thing in a vault, like a secret recipe.

But no, Rita pulled up Google maps just to be sure and it was just a normal, upper-crust neighborhood.

Judging by what Rita could see from the satellite maps, it seemed to be like any of her other upper-class marks. Her daytime reconnaissance in her shifter form outside the home also didn't reveal anything odd, though she checked to make sure there were no kid toys in the backyard.

She didn't like taking from families with kids, even if the parents could sometimes deserve it.

In a normal circumstance, she'd discuss the job with her client to find out if there was anything else she should know about the owner and the danger that might be waiting for her. Rita knew better than to try to follow up with her new boss, though. She'd annoyed the woman enough and was lucky to get the note at all. If the witch didn't want to leave her extra information, then Rita was going to have to just make it work.

Rita took a breath, sat at her computer, and had to really think about this.

What did she really know about this woman? Aside from the description and personality, she didn't know for *sure* if this was the famed matchmaker.

The mystery aspect was concerning, but it matched all descriptions, and Rita wouldn't be in the stealing game if a little uncertainty drove her away.

If she did this, she could find her soul mate.

Not just whoever was nice and good to her, but it would be the guy who was the absolute best for her. Her true love. No spending years with bad dates, wasting time in relationships that could take years off her life before ending in heartbreak.

Yeah, she was doing this.

When the date finally arrived, Rita was as ready as she could be. She staked out the place in her shifter form a few more times, seeing no movement in or out of the house all day. By nightfall, she was convinced that no one lived or worked there at all.

Under cover of dusk, she made her way to the second-floor windows. Big houses that were over two stories tended to get a little sloppy with the locks on anything above the first floor. That wasn't the case here. She checked every single window, and not a single one of them was unlocked.

Not uncommon.

The fact that they all had bars on them was the weird bit. There were padlocks on the outside in addition to the regular locks on the inside.

Were these people paranoid or were the crime statistics in this area worse than she'd thought?

She touched one of the locks with her little claws. Even if she were to pick the padlock, she'd still have to deal with the inside locks.

Rita shivered, the cold vibe of those places gripping her tight.

What the fuck was wrong with this house?

There had to be something pretty important in there for the witch to want her to steal from it.

And now, Rita's interest was piqued.

Whatever this was, it was big.

Damn, even if the witch woman hadn't sent her there, Rita would want to take a look inside anyway.

Rita scaled the wall, checking the third floor. The same deal. Windows locked from the inside and out.

She shuddered beneath her gray and black fur. Fear, curiosity, excitement, and adrenaline pushed her forward.

She loved this feeling. This was what she worked for. There had to be a way inside. There was always a way inside.

While Rita looked, she also plotted her potential escape routes. A woman without an escape route was like a damsel tied down to train tracks, and Rita was going to make damn sure she was never hit by that train.

She made use of the gutters to climb the rest of the wall until she made it to the roof. At some of her bigger jobs, security was stationed on the roof, but just as no one had gone in or out of the building all day, there had been no movement on the roof. There were times when she had missed things, though, so she made another quick check. Nope, no one was up there.

There usually weren't, but it was always safer to check.

Rita skittered along the roof, searching. Searching. Searching.

There was always an entrance. *Always.* If not a man-made one, then perhaps one made by rats or other animals.

She was in luck. There was an air vent that would work for her.

Also a door.

Rita loved choices.

First, she looked for cameras.

There were two of them, and they were both covered by those annoying little tinted domes that prevented her from knowing which direction they were pointed.

That was a special kind of pain in the ass, and it was going to take something of a risk for her to deal with them, but deal with them, she would. She wasn't getting into that vent without unscrewing the cover.

To unscrew the cover, she would have to get into her human shape.

To get through the door, she would also have to get into her human shape.

So she needed to deal with the cameras and hope to God they didn't catch sight of her face.

Rita ran beneath one of the cameras, banking on the fact that it likely would not be able to see directly beneath it.

She shifted quickly, shrugging off her little backpack that held her catsuit, mask, gloves, ballet flats, phone, and some small supplies, including her lock-picking kit. The bag camouflaged into her fur, and only added a little bulk that would make the casual observer think she was just a bit of a chunky raccoon.

The pack also held a small bottle of paint, necessary for situations just like this.

Rita reached up, high over her head, gently giving three small spritzes of dark blue paint to the dome. Anyone who happened to walk by wouldn't notice it right away, unlike the time she'd experimented with neon pink, thinking that would make for an amazing calling card.

She'd learned the hard way that was not the smartest idea in the world.

Neon drew attention to itself; that was the whole point. Sometimes her desire for fun overrode her common sense.

The camera most likely aimed at the door was no longer a problem.

So far, so good. Rita got to work on picking the door lock.

She had to be fast. If anyone was monitoring the camera, they'd soon be making their way up to see what was going on.

The other camera was far enough away and not in a clear line of sight, so she didn't waste any of her precious time with it.

This was why she hated paranoid rich people.

Who the hell needed so many cameras on top of their roof anyway? Despite the cameras and the double-locked windows, Rita could rely heavily on the fact that a lot of rich people got incredibly cheap at the most convenient spots. The door lock being a prime example. She had it open and was inside in just a few seconds.

She gave her eyes a moment to adjust to the near-blue glow and saw that she wasn't in an attic like you'd expect in a normal house. She was in a cement stairway, one you'd see in a commercial building.

She shivered when the warm air from the night gave way to the cold air conditioning. Much colder than it should be in a home.

She listened but heard nothing. It all gave her an eerie feeling.

Watching *Dawn of the Dead* last night had been a mistake.

Rita descended the stairs, keeping an eye out for any zombies who might stumble around the corner, spot her, and chase her back up the stairs.

But that was stupid.

Lots of strange things happened in this world; she'd even heard of aliens. But not zombies.

She'd checked.

Having already memorized the layout of the home, Rita knew exactly where the room was and which way she needed to go. As she made her way through, she spotted more annoying little camera domes and spritzed them when she could reach them. If she couldn't reach them, she didn't worry about them. There was no point in making a shift so she could get to them.

Sometimes it was best to duck down low and keep moving.

It was strange. The more she explored the house, the more she realized it didn't look much like a house. There was no carpeting, no paintings on the walls. The ceilings had fluorescent lamps illuminating the halls, instead of soft yellow scone lights that would be more appropriate in such a fancy place.

The more she saw, the more downright clinical everything appeared.

It smelled that way, too. It had the weird bleachy smell that made her think that some evil scientist could be performing experiments there.

And that freaked her out.

Where the hell had the witch sent her?

She kept going, though. Rita didn't back out of jobs, especially not because of a little fear. Besides, her interest way outweighed her unease.

Sometimes Rita honestly thought she should have been a cat shifter, based on how curious she was about everything.

Soon enough, she could see the door to her destination —the portal between her and the thing she was supposed to steal.

This door was more difficult to get through. But Rita was prepared for that. In addition to a high-tech lock, which required a little app on her phone to hack it, there was also a fingerprint scanner.

Hoping her tape trick would do the job, she covered her index finger with one of the pieces from her pack and pressed. If she messed this up, then an alarm would likely sound, and numerous guns would come her way. She didn't think turning into a raccoon and scuttling off would be enough to save her ass at this point.

The app finished its job, and the lock clicked green. Rita let out her breath when the fingerprint scanner also turned green. The adrenaline high hit her as the door clicked open.

She grinned.

She pushed it open to a whoosh of air. It sounded like she was entering the airlock of a spaceship. She stepped inside, and instead of seeing gold bars, jewelry, or even tapes that were loaded with all kinds of hideous information that could be used for blackmail, what she saw was...

A robot.

CHAPTER

TWO

Dallas was set to sleep mode, but something in the room caused him to stir. With his eyes closed, he heard the door click open, and he felt the pressure change when someone new entered.

And by new, he meant new to him. This person didn't have the biometrics of any of his usual keepers.

"Holy shit, it looks so real," he heard the voice say.

A soft voice. A woman's voice.

She suddenly sounded flustered.

"There's no way... how does she think I'm going to get this out of here?" He debated if he should just ignore her and wait for her to leave, but the mention of getting him was enough for him to boot up his system.

He heard the woman wander around the room, around the table he was strapped to, and around the machines he was hooked up to. He heard her opening cabinets and drawers, cursing as she talked to herself about finding something for a buyer? A witch?

"Hello?" The voice asked, closer to him now. He could answer, but he wanted to observe first. And then the woman did something unexpected. She touched a finger to his cheek.

"You're warm. Your metal cheek still feels like flesh."

And then she leaned in...

And sniffed him.

"You smell alive..."

And she smelled divine.

A small moan escaped Dallas's throat, and the woman let out a squeak and jumped away from him.

He opened his eyes in time to see her bang into the metal cabinets behind her. He automatically lurched forward, wanting to help her steady herself, but he was still bound to the table.

He caught her looking at the restraints, and he swore he could see relief in her eyes.

Did she think he was going to hurt her?

"Is this a trap?" She asked. "Why would that damn woman want me to be strangled to death by a creepy robot?"

He winced at the words she used to describe him. Not only was he not a murderer, but he also wasn't a creepy robot.

At least, he didn't want someone to think he was. Especially not this woman.

The woman saw his features change, and hers softened. "You're not a robot, are you? You're alive?"

He nodded carefully. He was pretty sure he was still alive.

"Are you a prisoner? I think maybe a friend of yours sent me to free you?" She cautiously approached the table again.

He tried to answer, but his voice failed him. A wispy breath left his mouth instead.

He hadn't spoken in so long. The woman's pitying expression returned. "Can you speak?"

He didn't want her pity. Dallas cleared his throat, trying again. "Yes." His voice came out sounding strained, with a crackling, almost static sound from the back of his throat. He coughed a little, and the snow sound vanished. "Who are you?"

"Name's Rita. And I think I'm the one that's getting you out of here." She looked down at him, making him aware that his black boxer briefs were the only thing he was wearing, and that they left little to the imagination. "Do you have anything to wear?"

"Negative, but if you release me, I have no problem running naked."

And he would do just that if it got him the hell out of here.

He couldn't leave her behind, however. If she was here, she was in danger as well.

"Do you need help escaping?" he asked.

Rita inhaled a deep breath, her eyes popping wide. "Right, so definitely a prisoner of some sort," she said, noticeably not accepting his offer of help.

He watched her pull out a tiny black kit and use the sticks inside to unlock the shackles that held down his wrists and ankles. Quick. Efficient. Before she finished the last one, she paused, looking up at him with a soft, careful smile. "I mean, I guess I could at least confirm first. Do you plan on doing me any harm once you're free?"

He shook his head. "I will not harm you. If you grant me freedom, I'll give you anything you want."

It took her just a few seconds of consideration before she nodded, easily convinced it seemed, and the last shackle popped open. "Lucky for you, the person who sent me here has the only thing I want." She smiled brighter this time, warming something in his chest. Dallas noticed something wistful in her gaze before her focus returned to him, worried once more. "You've got some tubes in you. Do I need to worry about those?"

"Tubes?"

He glanced around, trying to activate his memory. They did tend to hook him up to things while they worked on him. It's not like they bothered to inform him of what they were doing each time.

"That machine, right there," he nodded toward the main one, connected to a generator, beeping softly. "Pull the tube out and get it away from me."

She moved to follow his orders but hesitated when she saw that one of the tubes was latched into his neck. "You want me to pull this out?"

"Pull it out first, or turn the machine off first; I really don't care. Just need to get it away from me." His voice cracked a little. The desire to be free of the machine was strong. The realization that he was going to get out of there was overwhelming.

This was real. This was happening.

Rita moved to the machine first. Finding the button that turned it off, her hand hovered over it before she continued her questioning. "What is all of this? And why are you here?"

Irritation flared inside him. "Why do you ask so many questions?" Even as he said the words, he knew that the situation was a strange one.

It seemed the woman wasn't given any background on the situation. It was reasonable for her to be curious, but he didn't want to take any time to go over it. He wanted his body liberated from what they were pumping into him.

He'd tell her whatever she wanted to know while fresh, natural air was filling his lungs.

"Because if there is a chance you're dangerous, I probably shouldn't risk taking you out of here."

"If I were dangerous, wouldn't I have attacked you the moment you unshackled me? If my little robot brain was programmed to kill, wouldn't my arm have thrust out immediately to crush that smooth little neck of yours?" He spoke through gritted teeth, trying to hang on to his patience before he did turn into some kind of Frankenstein's monster and tear up the whole room.

Rita shrugged. "Maybe, but not everyone who is dangerous is instantly violent. Maybe you a more covert kind of threat."

"I'm here because I signed up to be here. Will you turn off that fucking machine now, please?"

Her hand faltered. She didn't press the button. "Why don't *you* turn it off?"

He no longer liked this woman. "I *can't*."

And he'd tried. Many times. Something about what was done to him stopped him every time, and it wasn't just the chord in his neck. That he could move around with him with enough effort.

It was something else.

Rita shook her head. "No way I believe that. No *way* you signed up to be strapped to that table, or whatever that is."

He rolled his eyes, letting his head bang against the metal table while he looked up at the ceiling, hoping she would put an end to this soon. "Look, I don't know how long I've been asleep. I'd all but given up on the hope of getting out, yet you show up saying you might help. Please, just get the thing out of my neck before it starts pumping again."

He heard a loud beep and looked to see she'd turned the machine off. Its steady red light had blinked off. His heart jumped. He looked at Rita, seeing her face still scrunched in uncertainty, but he'd take it.

"Thank you." He started to remove the wires and tubing from his body. "Can you help me out of this now, please?"

"Just to let you know, if you are a psychopath, you should be aware that I have superhuman strength and have been known to crush skulls with my bare hands."

He eyed her dainty frame. She had some lovely curves, but her wrists and ankles were thin. He detected not much in the way of physical strength in her. "Uh-huh."

She looked sharply at him, and he saw her dark eyes almost burning with a strength he hadn't expected. There was a passion in there, something attractive, something intriguing. Between that and his elation at being released from the table, he did something abrupt, something there wasn't time for, and he didn't have permission to do.

He kissed her.

It had been so long since he'd felt the press of a beautiful woman's lips on his mouth.

A woman he wanted, at any rate.

She didn't scream or shove him back. Always a good sign. Though he half expected her to be outraged by the sudden move.

No. Her warm body melted against him when their lips touched, full breasts flush against his naked chest. Invigorated, Dallas wound his arms wound around her, pulling her even closer. She opened her soft lips and let him deepen the kiss, meeting his tongue while his hands caressed the curves of her waist and hips.

Dallas hadn't held the flesh of a woman like that in too long, and this woman had a shape to be worshiped.

Her eyes were a touch glassy when they came up for air, her lips and cheeks a rosy shade of pink that hadn't been there before.

"Make you feel better?"

He grinned. "Yes, actually."

"Hmm," Rita nodded, making no move to leave his arms. "If you behave, I might let you do that again."

He wanted to kiss her again *now*.

She tasted, and felt, like nothing he'd ever had before.

And, for whatever reason, she was willing to return the touch and kisses of a half-naked man in a vampire's secret lair, so why not?

Her throat was warm and soft against his mouth. He grazed his teeth there, this strange, almost feral sensation at odds with the mechanical programming inside him.

Good to know he was still a flesh and blood man.

"We... we should get out of here before someone comes." Rita spoke breathlessly when he moved from her neck to her collarbone. He knew she was right, but he didn't care. All thoughts of freedom had left his brain because his body demanded to hold onto this woman. If he could sink deep into her, then it would be worth going back to the table.

He made a disagreeing sort of grunting noise.

"I'm serious," she said, even as her fingers tickled his lower abs, threatening to go lower. "We have to..." he caught her lips again. "Think of..." He hoisted her up, using his strength to hold her while she wrapped her legs around him.

Right when he was about to tear the fabric keeping them apart, a small beeping sounded from her little furry backpack. Her eyes went wide, and this time, she pushed him away with a force that indicated she *meant* it this time.

"That's my warning alarm. We have to get the hell out of here. I've been in too long."

With a massive ache in his balls and a disgruntled huff, he let her down and followed her to the door. They both eyed it. "It's locked," he said.

"It's fine." She pulled out her phone and poked around on it, then waited.

"What are we wait—"

She held up a finger, signaling for him to be quiet, then he heard the door click. He thought everything was going perfectly until she opened the door and they heard the sound of sirens.

CHAPTER

THREE

Oh, fucking Christ.

Rita felt the bottom of her stomach burn away.

She had fucked up. Of course she did. Because every once in a while, something shiny caught her attention, and it always screwed her over.

If only that witch had told her the thing she was going to steal was a gorgeous cyborg man, then she might not have found herself distracted and soon to be caught.

"How well can you defend yourself?" The man rubbed his wrists and rolled his shoulders. His eyes gleamed. He looked like a wild animal instead of a cyborg. As though he were getting ready for a fight.

Rita doubted he was ready for that. Who knew how long he'd been asleep, and they'd just pulled all those tubes out of him. Wouldn't there be muscle atrophy?

She eyed his shoulders, the plump curve of his effortless bicep, and those beautiful, solid abs...

Maybe muscular atrophy wouldn't be a problem.

Rita shook herself. "I need to get outside. I can shift."

He looked at her with more interest. "You can shift? Perfect! Are you a wolf? No, wait. You look more like a lioness. Between the two of us, I believe we can take them on."

"I'm a raccoon shifter."

Rita could see the change in his body when she said it. The non-metal skin that was already so pale seemed to whiten as the blood drained right out of him. Considering how much of him was currently robotic, it was actually kind of impressive.

"A raccoon shifter?"

Rita could *taste* his disappointment.

"Are you... serious?"

"Shut up. We have to get out of here." Rita reached for his hand and pulled him through the door without thinking. She wasn't sure why she had to grab him and lead him out, but now that she held onto his fingers, she did not dare let go. She had come this far to steal him out of here, and she was not about to leave him behind.

He didn't make any complaints, and there was no need to as they ran. Especially when people in black suits intersected them at a corner.

Their guns were the most worrisome part of them, and Rita immediately reached into her pockets for her secret weapons.

"Don't breathe this," She told him as she grabbed a few tiny vials. She slammed them onto the ground at the enemy's feet as she and her catch ran ahead.

Tear gas.

It was the most useful weapon she had on her. Rita never went on a mission without it. More than once it had saved her fuzzy ass, so if nothing else could be taken with her, then she always made sure she had a vile of the stuff on her.

The problem was how it seemed the men in black suits ran right through the smoke without slowing down.

Oh shit. Oh shit. Oh shit.

"If you've got some tricks up your sleeve," Rita huffed. "I'd be more than happy to see them."

Her new cyborg friend said nothing. She glanced at him, about to say something else, but she saw that he'd reached his hand back, the metal one, not the human-looking one. He held his wrist bent, palm facing the men chasing them.

Then, to Rita's disbelief, blue lights crackled on his fingers. A ball formed on the tips and grew larger to outgrow his palms before it shot toward their enemies.

Rita stumbled and actually stopped running as a beam of light rocketed down the hallway. The guards shouted and tried to duck out of the way. Some of them made it. Others didn't.

In horror, Rita watched as three people were launched backward all the way down the hall under the force of the light.

She smelled burning, but thankfully, she did not see any limbs go flying or blood spraying anywhere.

Rita tried to wrap her head around the kind of technology that would have made something like that happen. Something powerful, enough to take multiple grown adults out of the equation, and fantastical enough that it shot right out of a man's hand.

What the fuck did she steal?

Who did she steal?

"Who the hell are you?"

The man smiled, and her stomach did a melting thing.

"I'm Dallas. I'll answer all the questions you want after we get out of here. Come on!"

This time he grabbed her hand and led her down the hall and around the corners. She had no idea if he knew where he was going, especially considering she barely knew where *she* was going.

"We can't run out the front doors. They'll be expecting that," he shouted as they turned down another hall.

"I know. I know." Rita could swear that some of these hallways were not in the maps that she had memorized. That was not good. The last thing she needed was to be thrown off her game when trying to make a great escape. She needed to keep her focus. There were a few rooms that would provide a speedy escape, and Rita racked her brain to try to remember where they'd been on the floor plan, and how she could get to them now.

The second she realized where they were, she squeezed Dallas' hand and pointed the way. "That room! Right there."

"What?"

Thankfully he didn't fight her as she burst through the door and slammed it shut behind them.

"The desk! Push it in front of the door!"

Rita was glad Dallas had all those muscles and all those mechanical parts. They clearly enhanced his strength. The large mahogany desk must have weighed five hundred pounds easily, but it screeched across the floor. Dallas moved it with seemingly no effort. He'd broken more of a sweat when they made out earlier.

Dallas slapped his hands together and looked at her. "Right, what's the plan?"

"Quickie on the desk?"

He looked confused but interested. "What about the guards?"

Rita laughed, "I'm joking." Sort of. Because she certainly wanted him, whatever he was. She doubted he was a robot because he'd kissed her and responded to her body like a man.

She shook herself out of it. Now was not the time, even if it was jokes. "Right, yeah, the window."

"The windows are locked from the inside and outside and shatterproof."

Rita shivered. If he knew that, it was likely he'd learned it the hard way at some point. How long had he been here?

How many times had he tried to get out?

She grabbed the heavy curtain and pulled it aside, revealing the padlock on the inside of the window, and then pointed to the outside one. "Picked and ready to go. I unlocked the outside before I broke in."

She pulled out her tools and got to work on the inside padlock.

"You...just came in here, picked a few locks, and we're getting out? Just like that?"

"Yup, just like that," she said, totally faking how calm and collected she was.

The more she stayed in the damned house, the more freaked out and desperate she became to leave it.

Someone had done this to Dallas. She didn't know the full extent of it, but she knew that she didn't want to be caught. She didn't want anyone trapping her for who knows how long to experiment on her with who knows what.

Her fingers started to shake when a banging on the door started. It had been a long time since her hand had trembled while picking a lock.

This wasn't the good sort of adrenaline she strived for. This was something meaner and way more terrifying.

"How long do you need?" Dallas asked while standing at her back, putting himself between her and those trying to get in.

"A few seconds."

The sound of wood splintering caught her attention. They were smashing their way through and pushing hard enough to make the desk shift.

"Do what you need to do, and I'll hold them off."

"What? Wait!"

Too late.

He rushed towards the door, charging at it like an animal, and slammed his hands into it just as one of the guards stuck half his body through.

Dallas didn't let up as the man screamed, crushed under the weight of the barricade. He reached his metal arm out and grabbed the guy's skull, smacking it into the door frame.

Dallas released the first man when a new arm pushed through the small opening with a gun. Dallas grabbed onto it just as it shot.

Rita screamed a little, ducking her head, even though she had no idea where the bullet had landed. "Can't you do that blue shocky thing again? That seemed to work before!"

"No, I need to recharge. Pick the lock! Come on!"

Rita snapped out of it. He was right. Taking a deep breath, Rita tried to work through the trembling of her hands. Her composure was slipping fast.

She wasn't used to this. She wasn't used to the violence or guns being popped off. Her job was to sneak in, take what she wanted, and sneak out before anyone knew there was a problem. She didn't do confrontations like this, and she would have been happy to keep it that way.

No man in the world would make up for this, perfect mate or not. Nothing was worth this, and she couldn't believe her faith in some random witch's matchmaking skills had convinced her to do this.

Hell, at this point, she wasn't even certain that the note had been from the same woman. She should have done more to verify it.

But then, success! The lock popped open. The window was heavy and took some effort to move, as though the wooden frame had swelled into place over years of disuse. Finally, Rita got it open.

"The window's open. Let's go."

She was never coming back to this house after this. No secret, no matter how juicy, was worth the danger. At this point, when she was finished, she might hang up the whole thieving thing for good.

"Up there!" A voice from below shouted, pointing a flashlight up at her.

She froze. The light in her eyes caught her off guard, and then something painful hit her, as though she had been punched in the shoulder.

So tired. Her body melted. Unable to hold herself up, she fell. She didn't lose consciousness, however, not even as she landed on the grass and rock below.

The fall should have hurt. It was impossible for grass to have softened her landing. Falling from a second-story window was never a fabulous experience. Not even when she did it on purpose.

But it didn't hurt. Her body didn't scream in pain. She was barely aware she'd struck the ground at all.

Rita was perfectly aware of the men coming to stand

around her, their black shoes surrounding her. Her brain was turning to mush, so it was difficult to make out their words.

But she could understand the sound of screaming perfectly as they suddenly ducked away from her and tried to run.

She heard Dallas next.

At least, what she thought was Dallas.

He was chasing them off?

With her blurred vision, she could see him grabbing at the men before they even had time to point their weapons. He threw one of the men into a group of others, then broke another man's arm.

She heard more screaming and smelled the coppery scent of blood.

But Dallas was getting farther and farther away from her.

Wait, no!

No, no, no. She couldn't move. She couldn't get out of there. She needed Dallas to help her. He couldn't leave her behind. She was a sitting duck. If he didn't come back, the people who owned the house would have her.

Please come back. Don't leave me here. I can't move.

She tried to call out to him, to tell him she couldn't get out without him, but she wasn't so sure she said anything at all. More black boots stepped near her. She thought she felt another prick in her shoulder, and then the world started to fade even more.

Blacking out?

She was turned onto her back. A few shadowy figures looked down at her. She tried talking to them. She wanted to beg for some mercy, but no sound could leave her throat.

A bout of unconsciousness, and then she was aware of her body moving and swaying. She was being carried.

Back into the house. Where she would be experimented on and chopped up just like Dallas.

That bastard. Left her behind. Never should have gone for him.

"That's not very nice, but don't worry, I understand."

CHAPTER

FOUR

Dallas' escape, or rescue, however you looked at it, was hampered by Rita's capture. He could have left her behind. He could have headed off to his new life, stayed hidden forever, never to see that place of horrors again.

But he wasn't the kind of man to leave debts unpaid.

He beat down the first wave of guards, then faced another group that was coming from the back of the house. By the time he had them taken care of and circled back to Rita, a new lot had circled her.

He didn't know how many guards were around, but by the time he was done, he'd either taken them all out or scared them away.

It was only when Rita's eyes snapped open the following morning that he felt any relief.

She shot up, looking around as though searching for danger.

"You're awake." He couldn't think of what else to say. *Thank God you're okay* seemed over the top for someone he'd just met.

Rita snapped her attention to him. "Where are they?"

"Who? The guards?" Dallas gestured around them. "I took care of them last night."

Rita sighed and leaned back against the thick pine tree. "Where are we? I can hear water... smell it." Her words were stilted, and he could understand why. The tranquilizers were still ebbing out of her bloodstream, and she had had quite the fall. As Dallas thought of the infernal needles, Rita reached for her injured shoulder. It had taken not only the first dart but also the brunt of her fall. A small pained noise escaped her.

"Oh God," she groaned. She pulled her hand away, and Dallas saw the blood on her fingers that had soaked through her black shirt and her jacket. She looked at the blood, horrified, and then back to her shoulder.

"Here, let me help you." He pulled back her jacket and shirt. He had done some patchwork on the wound.

"You bandaged me with leaves?" She croaked.

"I mean, I used it as a compress till it stopped bleeding. Hey, you don't want to do that."

"Curious raccoon here, remember?" She said as she peeled back the compress. "I have to look."

"You landed on the dart, so it jabbed in pretty fucking deep and made the wound wider than it should have been."

She sighed and pressed the leaves back, holding them there to allow the new blood flow to clot.

"Here, take a drink." He offered her a small red bucket, something that had probably belonged to a child.

She took the plastic pale and stared into it, then looked at him.

"If I wanted you dead, I could have left you to fend for yourself."

Rita nodded. "True enough. But where did you get this water?"

"From the well. We're at a campsite, so it's good water. I didn't get it from the river, but I don't think that's anything you need to worry about either."

"We're on campgrounds?"

"Yeah, but we're not supposed to be. Now that you're awake, drink up so we can get moving."

"I was wondering where you got the clothes," she said between gulps. She poured some of the water into her hand and let the cold trickle over her hot shoulder. He watched her press her lips together, hissing at the pain.

"Does it hurt much?"

"Yeah, I think I should see a doctor."

"You definitely need stitches. I would have taken you, but it's better to hide and lay low for a while."

"Yeah, good thinking coming here. How did you get us here? These campgrounds aren't exactly close to where we came from."

"You've been out a while. I couldn't leave you behind, and this place was wide open, but we need to leave soon. I didn't exactly pay to get us on this spot, and these aren't exactly my clothes." He hooked his fingers into the collar of his new plaid shirt and a white T-Shirt.

She smiled. "You took those from someone?"

"Not because I wanted to. I'm not a thief."

Her smile vanished, and she looked away from him, though he didn't know why. She seemed insulted, but they didn't have time for him to figure out what she was thinking. "We need to get up and get going before the campers start waking up and a few people notice they've got some missing laundry. Can you walk at all?"

Rita nodded, pushing herself to her feet. "It's just my shoulder."

"You need help," he said, offering her his hand. Rita

nodded. Despite her determination to appear strong, she took his arm and put more weight into it than he thought she would. He was relieved that she did. Not only did he not want to fight her to allow him to help, but he also found he *liked* touching her.

He'd waited for her to wake up for hours. He knew it was sheer luck that had prevented them from being spotted by a campground official or a camper. Two people without a tent were definitely suspicious.

"I suppose you did save me from the guards. And you could have left me here and taken off. What's leaning on you just a bit more?"

He wanted to tell her that it was nothing. She'd helped him escape from his prison. He owed her so much—his life, even. Not to mention, there was something more. He felt something for her, and he had to figure out if it was the freedom high or if the thing he felt toward her was real.

Dallas set the red pail down on the ground, hoping the child he'd taken it from would find it when they woke up.

Then they walked out. Just like that.

"We're going to pretend to be campers taking an early morning stroll if anyone happens to see us? That it?" She asked.

"Yup. Hopefully, no one *else* sees us."

"Has anyone seen you so far?"

"A few people. I think they were a little nervous to stop and question me, though."

"Right, I guess it would be hard to ask you what you were up to."

"Yeah, can't exactly blend in anymore."

It was the first time she mentioned his appearance and the first time he'd thought about it since being out. He was so focused on not getting caught for unauthorized camping that he'd not even thought about how someone might take his metal limb and enhancements. It was weird. He still felt like himself; he still felt like a man. Would he ever get used to being more than that? Would he ever automatically remember what the outside world saw when they looked at him?

The shirt he wore covered most of his metal arm but didn't hide the metal plating on the side of his hand. Nothing would cover the metal that made up a good quarter of his face.

They made their way to the trails. They walked like a couple taking an early morning stroll to remain as inconspicuous as possible.

The only thing missing was the dog. If they had a golden retriever, it would be perfect.

"So, you wanna tell me what brought you to Lilly's house last night?"

"Lilly?"

He looked at her, surprised at her question. "You didn't know whose house that was?"

"I was hired to go in and do a job. Normally I would have information on the owner, but it didn't work out that way."

"You didn't do your research before conducting a rescue mission? Who are your partners?"

"I work alone."

"You work alone? Who does that?"

"The lady who saved your ass did it."

He was quiet for a moment. "I'm sorry, it's just unreal that I'm finally out of there. Even if I've got these to show for it." He flexed his metallic fingers.

"Did you have...your hands before? I mean, were you..."

"Normal?"

"I wasn't going to say it like that."

He smiled softly, though it wasn't even close to being a happy smile. "I had all my fingers, all my toes, everything you look for when hiring a security team member."

"So... Lilly cut your arm off? She did this, put all this on you?"

He nodded. "She did."

"And you said you signed up for that?"

"I didn't sign up for her to cut my arm off and take out part of my skull, but I was working for her."

"You worked for her? You were one of those other men, the people in black and the guy who shot me down from the window?"

"I was." He should have been annoyed by all of the questions, be he liked them, coming from her. She was curious and not ashamed of it. He found that endearing.

"She's willing to turn you and all of her employees into cyborgs, and you all still want to work for her?" "

He shrugged. "Makes it seem extra stupid when you put it like that."

"It is stupid! What the hell were all those guys thinking?"

Dallas pointed to a woman walking a dog coming toward them, indicating that they should keep their voices down. They didn't want to draw any more attention to themselves than necessary.

Rita lowered her voice to a whisper. "They could all be in that same position you were in. If this woman is that rich and powerful, she could do to them—"

"Exactly what she did to me. I know that, and they know that. It's why they still work for her. They don't want to be in my position."

"So, they're trapped, too?"

"In a way," Dallas admitted. "I worked for her long after I knew it wasn't the right thing to do. People just get trapped."

"How? If you're free to leave, why wouldn't you do it?"

He shrugged. "The pay is half the battle. Some people have kids to feed. Others have massive debts they need to pay off. Lilly paid all of us very well for what we did for her. That money would stop coming if we walked away, and the ones that did were never able to work in their field again."

He looked at her again. "The threat of not being able to work again, even for a shitty pay, is just as detrimental as the worry about having food on the table for your kids."

"I know, I just... if it was that bad..."

"A frog in slowly boiling water will sit still until he boils to death," Dallas said. "Put that same frog in an already boiling pot, and he'll jump out immediately."

"You're saying your old friends back there are boiling frogs?"

"That's exactly what I'm saying."

"You didn't have to kill any of them, did you?"

"No," he shook his head but didn't smile. "Broke enough arms that they're not going to be working for a while."

"It's better than being dead."

"They won't think so when they can't pay for their kid's piano lessons or whatever. They were still my friends. They didn't want to come at me or keep me there any more than I wanted to throw them around like that. I didn't know I could until I tried it."

They were getting closer to the edge of the campground now. The bike trails were in sight, and just over the fence was likely where the edge of the land reached. More people were coming into sight. A few bikers. A jogger with his iPod strapped to his arm ran by, and his double-take when spotting Dallas' face was overtly obvious. If too many people happened to see them, they were definitely going to draw attention to themselves.

"Where will you go after this? Are you going to meet up with your friend?"

"Friend?"

She seemed confused. "You know, Esme. The witch?"

He looked at her, searching his own memory. "I don't know any Esmes or witches."

"What do you mean? I was sent here by one to..." Rita looked around, and when she saw no one was in listening range, she added, "She's the one who paid me to get you out of there."

Dallas shook his head. He was sure he wasn't imagining this. This couldn't be something else Lilly had taken from him. "I've never met any witches before. I have no idea what you're talking about."

Rita was confused.

He didn't know who the matchmaker was. He'd never met any witches before either? Ever?

This man, robot, cyborg guy had the chance to escape but had chosen to save her from shooters, bandaged up her wound, and sit vigil by her side until she regained consciousness. She thought that he'd probably done it because he needed her to take him to Esme, but now he was saying that wasn't the case.

Who the fuck was that woman?

Who was *he*?

"You helped me?"

He blinked at her like he wasn't understanding the problem. "I did."

Rita swallowed, a warmth fluttering and swelling in her chest.

This...complicated her feelings. She was trying not to let herself feel some kind of hero worship toward him, but it was hard. He'd saved her, and he had the good looks of a movie star. Square jaw, bright green eyes, thick eyelashes, and a muscle definition that would make the ocean king envious.

The metal plating around his eye and arm didn't bother her. It certainly hadn't put a damper on their brief make-out session the night before.

Rita suddenly felt warm, remembering how eagerly she'd returned his kiss and how close they'd actually come to going all the way.

She wasn't normally like that. She wasn't a prude, but generally, she liked to have dinner and a conversation before things got physical. She also generally liked to be in a bed of some sort. Maybe a public restroom, but never a house she was in the middle of robbing!

It had to just be the rush of the job, she tried to convince herself. The intense feelings from the night before were still there, though. It wasn't like her to let her guard down so easily. Just because she was an amazing raccoon shifter who could scratch the eyes out of anybody who tried to restrain her, did not mean she was all-powerful. This had been proven the night before, as she had been unable to get herself out of *that* particular pickle.

Why had she let this guy distract her?

And how was she going to explain that she wasn't some kind of rescuer, but a simple thief sent to his location? Most people didn't look too kindly on those with her career choice, even if she was only doing it to the people who deserved it. Best to keep that from him for now. He'd brought her this far, and she didn't want to take the risk that he leave her behind when she still needed some help getting out of there.

Plus, her theory that the note had been sent to her from someone other than the witch held water. The proof was clear; Dallas didn't know who Esme was. She'd have to figure it out and might need him to help her with that too.

They got out of the campgrounds. No one stopped them. No other early-rising campers and no campground workers either. When they got to the highway, they stopped.

"I doubt anyone is going to give us a ride..." she stared. They both looked a mess.

"We both sort of look like something out of a horror movie," Dallas said, as if reading her mind.

"Guess we have to hope someone is dumb enough to take the risk on us, huh?"

Dallas' blue eyes flew wide.

Rita laughed, then had to quickly stop because it hurt.

They had only held out their thumbs for five minutes before they were proven wrong. Rita hadn't even needed to show extra skin. A trucker pulled to the side of the road for them.

As they got into the cab, the driver looked at them, keeping his eyes on Dallas for a few extra seconds before shrugging. "I'll take y'all down to the next gas station, a'ight?"

"That's perfect, thank you," Rita said.

Her trusty faux-raccoon fur backpack had stayed with her through it all, and she checked it to make sure she still had her little stash of money. Her phone, long dead, wouldn't be much help, but payphones were still a thing. Or so she hoped.

The thing she didn't expect to see? A business card.

A business card she didn't have before, sitting in her phone wallet.

There was no name, but the card was made of a soft, ivory glitter paper with hearts in the corner.

There was a phone number and a small handwritten note in a familiar black script.

Call me when you're ready, darling.

Jesus Christ. *Seriously?* How the fuck...?

Whatever. She wasn't going to question it. Everything was nuts today.

She just needed to get to a phone and get a taxi back home. Then she could try contacting the woman to ask what the hell was going on.

They were dropped off as promised. Rita was dying to use the toilet, wash her hands and face, and feel something a little closer to human. She checked out her wound in the bathroom mirror.

Then cringed.

Yeah, she definitely needed to get a shot for that. It was going to get infected if she didn't do something about it.

She was able to buy some painkillers with the cash she had on hand, but those tiny little packets only contained two pills each. They weren't going to last her long.

She'd be lucky if they did anything at all. Shifter genes made substances less effective for her kind.

Bit of a blessing in some cases, but definitely a curse whenever she wanted to get drunk.

She asked for some coins for the payphone and got a look from the cashier. "Battery's dead." She held up her cell as proof, and he shrugged, handing her quarters in exchange for her five.

First, she called for a cab. The fifteen-minute wait time didn't surprise her, but it did give her plenty of time to make a call. Rita was burning to know what the hell she'd gotten herself into.

She pulled out Esme's business card and dialed the number. It took a solid thirty seconds before the familiar voice of that damned woman finally picked up. Rita had been worried she'd be sent to voicemail and have to call her back, or worse, that this was someone else's card.

"Hello sweetie, how did the heist go?" The witch's voice was so chipper that Rita had to cool herself. Clearly, Esme had sent Rita to the house. She knew about the heist, but shouldn't she have been more concerned about Rita's well-being?

"How did you know it was me calling you? And can you help me to understand what's going on?" She made sure to word herself carefully. Shouting, *what the hell is going on?* wasn't respectful, and no matter what trials this lady might put her through.

"Why wouldn't I know it would be you? I've only been waiting for you to call all night."

Rita didn't think that made it so obvious, but she was going to go with it.

For now.

Rita turned away from the clerk, a tense smile for him as he raised a brow at her. She couldn't remember the last time she'd been wrapped up with a phone cord, but she didn't want to even look at the guy while talking to Esme.

Speaking low, she asked, "What did you send me into? There was a guy waiting for me."

There was a soft chuckle. "Yes, there was."

Rita was going to lose her careful patience very, *very* soon. "So what was I supposed to see?"

What did you want me to take? was the question she really wanted to ask.

"Exactly that. He's a cutie, isn't he?"

Rita couldn't believe it.

"You sent me there to... to pick up a guy?" She glanced over her shoulder.

The guy behind the counter had his nose stuck in his phone, scrolling in the usual way that social media addicts did. Even so, just because it didn't *look* like he was paying attention didn't mean that he wasn't.

"Not to *pick him up*. Of course, I'm the last person in the world to judge if you did want to have a nice pick me up."

Rita rubbed her eyes.

"I sent you there to rescue him."

Rita had to cover the speaker of the phone, whispering into it. "You didn't tell me I was going there to get a person. I might have prepared a little more if I had known that."

"I wanted to keep the surprise," she said, all innocent-like.

There didn't seem to be anything so innocent about this. "He's never even heard of you. I thought you only kept... *certain people* on your list." Rita thought of something else. "And how the hell did you get your business card in my bag?"

"I have my ways, and I do keep lists. Of shifters who want to find their fated mates."

"He looked pretty normal to me when I first saw him. Aside from the, uh, extras."

Talking about this in public was too difficult. It only got worse when more people came into the station to pay for their snacks and gas.

"Extras?" A sad note pulled at the woman's voice.

Rita rubbed the back of her neck, thinking about his arm, his face, and his skull. Part of his abdomen, even his lower left leg. "I don't think I can get into that here. There are too many people around."

"Get home quickly, dear. Give me all the details when you're done with your inspection."

Rita blinked. "Done? Done what? Don't you want me to bring him to you?"

"Of course not. Like you said, I keep no humans on my list. He's not my client. You are."

"Wait. What? Do you mean—"

"Details later, sweetie, bye!"

The phone went dead before Rita could get another word in. She stared at the receiver, wondering what the fuck had happened. She had no answers, only more questions.

"D'you need anything else?" asked the kid behind the counter. He really didn't give a shit, his tone suggested.

"Uh, no." She hung the receiver in the cradle. "Thanks for the change."

Rita glanced outside. Dallas was still there, standing at a distance, off in the shade of a tree. She could see him, but no one who glanced his way would notice there was something off about his face or his exposed hand.

The witch had sent her to collect him... because he was the one Rita would be matched with?

Really?

Rita hadn't been sent on a heist. It hadn't been a barter for services. It had all been a ploy to get Rita with her match. With Dallas. The knowledge rattled around in her head but failed to attach itself to reality or sense.

Rita knew it was possible for shifters to mate with humans. Of course, she didn't know if Dallas could still be called human now that Lilly had done the whole Robocop thing to him. But Rita *did* know that she'd had strange feelings since the moment she laid eyes on Dallas. It was common knowledge that shifters would know it the moment they saw their mate. Would it be possible for shifters to not recognize the feeling?

She wished that Goddamn woman would have just spelled it out for her. Love and mating were complicated, and Rita wasn't sure how she was going to explain any of it to Dallas.

"Do you need anything?" The kid asked again, clearly getting impatient.

Rita jumped. "Yeah, sorry."

She grabbed some bottles of water and beef jerky for her and Dallas, then went outside to wait for the cab with her match.

CHAPTER

SIX

They were quiet in the cab, not wanting the driver to overhear any strange conversation. Dallas wanted to ask what day it was, or what year, for that matter, but he held his questions for later.

He was surprised that Rita had taken him to her apartment. She'd been apprehensive about him before, so he'd figured she would have taken him to whoever his mystery savior was.

"We're going to your place? Not the hospital?"

"I need to get my car," Rita answered him, barely sparing him a glance as she paid the driver and headed into the building.

In her apartment, Dallas stood in the doorway, watching her scuttle around, plugging her phone into a charging hub, and then running to her room to change. "I'll just be a minute."

The place was cluttered and a bit messy, in an "I didn't expect to have company" way combined with an "I'm a little bit of a packrat" way. He wasn't turned off by it,

48

though. It showed character, giving him a clear glimpse of who Rita was.

In fact, spying the lacy red bra thrown over a chair, Dallas couldn't help but be a bit turned on. He smirked, wondering if he should pick it up and ask her about it, but then remembered that she was injured. They needed to get her patched up first, and then they could see about picking up where they left off. He looked at the bathroom door, imagining her naked behind it, and his cock stood at attention.

Good to know things are still in working order.

His thoughts were stamped out when she came out of the bathroom, her face dark.

"Are you okay?"

"I'm good," Rita said, grabbing her fur backpack and tossing some things into it, including some clothes, the phone, and its charging hub.

"You look kind of pale. Let's get you to the hospital."

"I'm good. It's just embarrassing to have you in my disgusting apartment."

He didn't pretend to fall for the lie.

"It's something else. What happened? You barely spoke a word to me since we got in the cab."

"A lot's happened. There's a lot to think about," which was true, but he still had the feeling there was something she wasn't telling him.

They headed back downstairs. Rita's apartment was on the third floor, and the elevator wasn't working. He'd wanted to carry her up the stairs, but she'd refused. At least going down would be easier.

That's what she said... Dallas was glad that his sense of humor hadn't been surgically removed by Lilly's experimenting.

He stroked the metal plating around his eye.

"Is there somewhere I can drop you off?"

"What?"

She looked back at him. "You must live somewhere, right?"

He thought about it, a slight sense of panic overcoming him when he couldn't immediately remember.

But then, no, he had something. Vague and far away in his mind, but it was there. His life before.

"You okay?"

Dallas exhaled a heavy breath. "Yeah."

His life before Lilly was there, and it was real. He could remember his parents and the place he lived. Or used to live. He doubted his place was still empty and waiting for him.

"Do you remember where you live?"

"I've been strapped to that table for nearly a year. Someone else probably lives there now."

"So she just, made you disappear?"

"Lilly ransacked my place to make it look like I left town." He could remember her showing him photos when he'd shouted at her that people would come looking.

She'd made sure no one would be looking for him. His parents were long dead, and he only had work friends, so a landlord or neighbors doing any searching was out of the question.

Some of those work friends... he'd trusted them. They helped tie him down and injected him with shit that put him out of commission for Lilly to do what she wanted.

It was fucking depressing

Dallas shook himself, not willing to cry like a bitch about it in front of the woman who saved him, and he didn't care where she came from or who sent her.

Far as he was concerned, he owed her.

"Anyway, I'm not going anywhere 'till I see you patched up."

She rubbed her head like she was getting a headache. "Why the hell do you have to be a Prince Charming?"

He cocked his head, fighting a smile at her ridiculous description of him. "You're clearly not a damsel, so if you think I'm doing this because I'm trying to take care of you, then you're wrong."

Rita crossed her arms, though she didn't appear defensive. "Then why are you doing it? You don't know me. You don't have to escort me to the hospital."

"It's not an escort. They saw your face. You broke me out of there, and I owe you. I won't walk away and let myself wonder if you were caught and taken hostage or killed by a damned infection." The very thought brought a new sense of urgency inside him. "So let's go. You can get rid of me later."

"Fine. But don't think this means anything."

"I know. I'm the one who owes you here. Let's go."

When they made it to the hospital, Dallas could tell that Rita was in more pain than before. A thin, swinging layer of sweat beaded on her forehead. Her jaw tightened as she clenched her teeth, but she seemed determined to not show her discomfort.

It made him want to take care of her all the more.

They both ignored the odd looks from patients and nurses, and we're glad that no one said anything.

When it was Rita's turn to be seen by the doctor, Dallas caught the "thank God" and the groan that escaped her as she stood to follow the nurse. She stumbled, almost fell, and Dallas had to catch her.

Her cheeks turned a deep shade of pink. He felt the

warmth in her body as he held her, though she refused to look at him. "Thanks."

"Don't mention it." He didn't want to embarrass her, but his stomach clenched at the thought of her being out of his sight, where he couldn't protect her.

"I'd like to go with her if I can," he stated, worried the nurse would say it was family only.

"Of course," the nurse said instead, and Rita seemed too weak to protest. In fact, her grip around his shoulders tightened.

Dallas helped her follow the nurse, worried at how little strength she seemed to have. The nurse looked tired but worried as she took Rita's vitals and assured them the doctor would be there shortly.

Twenty-five minutes later, the doctor still hadn't shown up.

Rita groaned. "Ugh. They should just put me out of my misery already."

Thankfully, the doctor finally came in. She had a clipboard in her hands and looked at Rita with a sorry smile on her face, as though this happened all the time. When she greeted Dallas, her eyes only grazed over him, showing no sign that she thought anything was strange about his appearance.

"Sorry for the wait. I understand you have a potentially infected puncture wound on your shoulder?"

"Yeah," Rita said, "Camping, a little bit of alcohol, and an accident with a barbeque skewer. Thought I could sleep it off."

Dallas wondered if the doctor actually bought the story.

"And your boyfriend didn't bring you in right away?" Dallas knew the doctor had to be wondering what his role was in the accident. Surely she didn't think he'd done that to Rita?

"Uh, no, Dallas is just a friend. He brought me here because he was worried about me. We're not together."

The doctor looked at her in a way that suggested she was debating whether or not to believe her. She must've decided it was all right to let it pass because then she shrugged and didn't ask for follow-up questions. Her face was grim when she peeled back the leaf compress. "I'm going to clean this up a bit so I can get a better idea of what's going on, okay?"

Dallas noticed Rita's breathing becoming more shallow when the doctor started prodding the wound. "Is she going to be okay?" He asked, making his way to the opposite side of the table and taking Rita's good hand.

"Of course, she's here now, and we're going to treat her. You should lay back, Rita. Are you light-headed?"

Rita nodded and laid back, her eyes closed but her grip still tight on Dallas' hand.

He stood by her side while she recoiled at the spraying of water on her wound. He sat in a chair and hovered over her, allowing her to bury her face in his neck when they gave her two needles and a couple of stitches. Then he pulled up a game on her phone for them to play for the thirty minutes she had to sit with an antibiotic IV drip.

By that point, Rita was looking a bit healthier. At least healthy enough to beat him in *Risk* and gloat about it. With a prescription for painkillers and a follow-up appointment, they left the hospital approximately three hours after they'd arrived.

Rita smiled and inhaled a deep breath when they exited the hospital. "Free at last." Right after the words left her lips, she faltered, looking guiltily at him. "I'm sorry, I didn't mean, well, to compare the hospital to what you went through."

"It's okay. You don't have to change how you speak now that you're in the company of a man you broke out of a vault."

"Shhh!" She raised a finger to her lips. "Rescue or no, I don't think folks will take kindly to knowing there's a thief in their midst."

She looked so scared when she said it, that Dallas thought she might actually feel like she'd committed a crime in rescuing him. "I think when they find out that you were stealing a person out of there, then they might be a little forgiving."

She sighed, seeming relieved, and they headed to her car. "You're going to follow me home, aren't you?"

"I'm going to drive you home if that's what you mean. I won't come inside if you don't want me to, but I'd really like to see you settled and with a real meal in your belly."

Dallas walked her to the building door, opening it for her, standing behind her while she walked up the stairs to make sure she didn't fall."What are you going to do? Now that you're out?" Rita asked as they made it to her floor.

"I'm going to pay Lilly a visit and put a stake through her heart."

"You say that like she's a vampire or something—" When Rita saw his face, she realized the truth of it. "Oh, I guess that explains why you all didn't have a better chance at escaping her."

Something drew his attention to Rita's apartment door. "Wait," he said, touching Rita's good shoulder and guiding her to pause before touching her door.

"What?"

Dallas leaned in close, so close to her ear that he could

feel the heat of her body. "Can't you hear them? You're a shifter."

In response, she stilled, cocked her head to the side, and closed her eyes. "Shit, yeah, I wasn't paying attention. Someone's in there."

"You waiting for someone?" Dallas asked, still keeping his voice so low that only Rita would hear him.

Rita shook her head. "No."

"Let's go then."

Dallas pulled her back towards the door to the stairs. They didn't make it a step before her door burst open, and three men in familiar black suits came rushing out.

SEVEN

Rita had just started to feel the effects of the drugs. She felt a little less pain, and her head felt clearer. She was even getting around to making the decision to tell Dallas the truth.

Explaining to him that some anonymous witch was setting them up and that she was a thief who'd been tricked into freeing him was a little more crazy than Rita was used to. She wasn't sure how to approach that.

The trip home had been a challenge. She'd already been awkward enough around him when they were trying to escape together. Despite all those metal implants, he was still unbearably attractive.

He was a sexy cyborg who had saved her when she'd been down and out for the count, as helpless as could be. Rita had a thing for guys like that.

She didn't like admitting it, not even to herself. There was something nice about a man who wanted to pound his chest and care for someone who needed it. And, to top it all off, a legendary matchmaking witch had *matched* them.

It was all made better because Dallas didn't want to

care for her because he saw her as a tiny, helpless woman or whatever. No. He wanted to help her because he felt indebted to her. He was honorable and wouldn't walk away, even if she was only a little injured.

That was the sort of person she liked best.

In her line of work, Rita had come across too many people who were only out for themselves. People who pretended to work with her, just to turn around and stab her in the back at the first sign of trouble. She hated people like that.

No one had felt loyalty toward anyone anymore. Sometimes Rita worried that she was falling into that same pit. That her chosen career would lead her to think only of herself.

She had almost fallen into that trap when escaping with Dallas in the mansion. She could have left Dallas in the horrible place and jumped out of the window to safety. She had been shot before making up her mind. This irked her. Now here Dallas was, insisting on following her and making sure she was all right when he didn't even know her.

None of that mattered, though, because they weren't able to enter her apartment, where they could have discussed their interactions and expectations. Where they could have had that dreaded conversation.

Dallas grabbed Rita's arm and yanked her so hard behind him that it jerked her already throbbing shoulder. She shouted from that pain, stumbled, and fell to her knees, but Dallas didn't seem to notice.

She looked up, and he was already on the three men, picking one of them up, and with a hard shout, throwing him at the other two.

They all went down perfectly, and Dallas turned back to get to her.

Rita, not wanting to look like she couldn't handle herself, shot to her feet quickly before he could reach her. That didn't stop him from grabbing her hand and pulling her into the stairwell just as they heard popping noises behind them.

"Holy shit. They're shooting at us," she breathed, though it didn't exactly surprise her.

She had been shot at before after stealing someone's property.

But Dallas wasn't property. He was a person, no matter how much metal he'd been replaced with. He was no one's property, and Rita was going to get back at those fuckers for shooting at them.

"We need to get out of here," she said.

The door behind them eventually opened up, but only after they made it to the first floor. More popping noises sounded, the noise amplified by the stairway. Metallic pings rang off when the bullets hit the stairs or the railing instead of their intended target.

"Holy shit!" Rita shrieked.

Dallas punched the door open. It looked almost as though he broke the hinges and the knob, but it was difficult to tell when they were running for their lives.

"Where are we going?" Rita asked.

"You need to shift and head into the trees. I'll draw them away."

"What?"

He shoved her ahead of him, directing her to make her break for the edge of the parking lot where the brush started up.

There were no heavy woods or anything like that near

her building, but there were enough trees and shrubs and lawns and houses everywhere that it would be easy enough for a raccoon to disappear.

"Go!"

She couldn't go. Rita clutched at her shoulder, but she didn't feel the pain anymore as she watched him turn back to face the glass doors of her building. The three men in suits came out running. Even with their agent-style sunglasses on, they were clearly pissed off from being thrown around.

"Don't make us do this, Dallas," one of them said.

"Keep away from me, and I won't, Bryce," Dallas said back.

With a shock, it occurred to her that these were probably Dallas' friends. These were the people he'd worked with before this had been done to him. He'd probably eaten lunches with them at work and maybe even met their families.

The threat of not being able to work again, for anyone, even for a shitty pay, is just as detrimental as the worry about having food on the table for your kids.

She could still remember those words coming out of his mouth and thinking to herself that it was no excuse to do what they were doing to him. That they were all monsters.

But they weren't. Dallas talked to them as if he knew them, and he talked about them as if he didn't blame them.

Which made this so much worse than she'd thought.

Friends fought each other because Lilly had all of them in her pocket.

Somehow, she felt sorry for them, but that didn't make them any less dangerous.

They'd still hand her and Dallas over to that vampire woman.

"Come on, man. This can go one of two ways. You know we don't want to hurt you."

"I don't want to hurt you either," Dallas said. "But I will if I have to. You want to go back to Marge with your nose inside out?"

Bryce's mouth thinned into a line. "And what about her? I like you, Dallas, but if you think for one second we can be nice to her for your sake, then you're out of your mind."

"You shut the fuck up and don't even look at her! You got me!"

It almost sounded like a growl came out of him. Something so animalistic shouldn't belong to a man with so many metal parts.

And Rita responded to it. She didn't want to mess with it.

The guys in black didn't seem to pick up on whatever it was.

That was normal with humans. They were often so blind to anything to do with nature, and these ones couldn't sniff out the danger even though it was right in front of them with its fists clenched.

Bryce didn't have a weapon in his hands, but when Rita really looked, she could see the two men behind him did have their guns out.

Were they real guns? Or more dart guns?

She didn't like the idea of either. Her shoulder started throbbing again at the idea of being shot with anything.

"Bryce, I mean it."

"So do I, Dallas. It's three against two, and she's injured, and both of you are unarmed. Stand down."

"Can't you just let us go?" Rita asked. "What's the vampire bitch gonna do to you if you let us walk away?"

"Rita, stop," Dallas said. He held his arm out and stepped in the way, blocking off her view from the three men.

No, he was blocking their view of her, trying to keep the attention of those three off her.

Bryce rubbed his jaw. He shook his head. "Lilly wants the both of you. She gets what she wants, Dallas. You know that."

"Yeah, I know that," he said. "Bitch used me as a blood farm, and you think I'll let you take me back alive?"

"I believe you will try to make us kill you before going back," Bryce said. "But then there will be no one left to keep her safe. Is she gonna kill herself to keep us from taking her?"

"Jesus Christ," Rita breathed, a cold shiver rippling down her spine.

Too much. This was way too much.

And she was getting angry.

So was Dallas.

"You motherfuckers. You sons of bitches. I can't even believe you're all doing this."

"Yes, you can," Bryce said. "Because you're exactly like us."

Bryce looked back at the two men behind him, gesturing with his hand in what looked to be a sign to keep their guns pointed down.

He reached out his hand to Dallas, as though offering a peace treaty. "Come on, man. Come in with us, and I swear I will do everything I can to convince Lilly to take it easy on the both of you. She your girlfriend or something?"

"She means nothing to me, so you might as well let her go."

"If you say she means nothing to you, Lilly will have us shoot her," Bryce said.

Dallas growled. "And if I tell you she's important to me, that bitch will get jealous and slit her throat in front of me!"

"It's over, man. Just surrender."

Dallas looked back at her, just a quick glance, but it was enough. His shoulders sagged. "Let her walk away. Don't follow her. She can pack up a bag, leave here, and you won't see her ever again. Let her do that, and I'll come in with you. No fighting and no trouble."

No. This wasn't right. "Don't let yourself be taken in because of me," Rita pleaded with him, touching his arm and meeting his bright green eyes. She couldn't let him go back into captivity because of her.

All those tubes in his neck and arms as he lay motionless on that table, strapped down. That would become his life again, while Lilly did what? Took his blood?

Rita still didn't understand the need to remove some of his limbs and replace them with extra parts, but what did she know about the mind of a crazy woman who tortured one of her bodyguards?

For all Rita knew, the bitch had done it for the fun of it, and now she had sent some of Dallas' friends after him to bring him back.

Once again, Rita was stuck wondering what in the hell she'd gotten herself into, but she knew for a fact that she wasn't about to let herself get used as a way to finish ruining Dallas' life.

Match or no match.

If she was going to help him, then she needed to get away. She'd have a better chance of helping Dallas from the outside than inside as a prisoner with him. Rita needed to take herself out of the equation since she was basically being used as a hostage.

"I want to go home. I don't want to be here," she said, keeping her voice small. She was already scared, so if playing up that emotion helped in her ability to look small, weak, and scared, then so be it. "I'm sorry. I didn't know whose house that was. I didn't mean to get involved. I want to leave. Please let me leave."

Dallas kept his fists clenched, though his expression softened. "Bryce, come on. I know you don't want to do this. Please don't do this. Let her go."

It seemed to be working. Not that Rita could read minds or anything, but even behind those sunglasses, she could see he was struggling.

It was in the way he glanced back at the two men who were with him. The way his mouth stayed firm, how he didn't respond right away.

"We can't just let her walk away," said one of the men behind him.

Bryce rubbed his jaw again.

"A trade-off then. You'll come quietly if she goes?"

"Bryce, come on, Lilly's gonna fucking kill us if we don't bring both of them back."

Not good. If the two guys were going to panic and rat out Bryce for wanting to help Dallas, then he just might not help him.

But Bryce was looking for an excuse to not take it so far. "If we tell her it was the only way to get Dallas to come in quiet, she'll understand. She wants his blood."

"She won't understand, and she's gonna rip our throats out, you stupid fuck!" Screamed the guy to Bryce's left. "I am not getting ripped apart and fed from because you don't know how to follow orders!"

Dallas looked back at her. He gestured for her to go.

Rita did. She didn't stop to think about it. Even with stitches in her arm, Rita didn't think she'd ever run so fast.

Turns out that a life-or-death situation really brought out her talents.

She vaguely heard the shouts of the men behind her. A few more guns popped off. She knew to zigzag, lowering her chances of being shot. She leaped into the shrubs.

CHAPTER

EIGHT

Dallas knew that Rita had been putting on a show. She was cagey, and obviously had some sort of plan. He wished she didn't. If she could just leave and get to safety, he wouldn't have to worry about her.

A few days ago, all he cared about was himself and getting freedom. But now he cared about Rita. He didn't know why the feelings were so intense, he didn't know why it felt like he'd known her his whole life, but he was absolutely certain that the most important thing to him was Rita's safety.

He'd take whatever Lilly would do to him so long as she left Rita alone.

His friends howled in anger as Rita ran, and Dallas went back to fighting them. They had their guns, but as long as he could stay between them and Rita, he didn't care how many holes they put in him.

Then they upped their game. Bryce pulled something from a sheath on his leg.

Dallas recognized the weapon. It resembled a light stick, but it was worse than that.

Bryce jammed it into Dallas' side, and Dallas screamed, falling to his knees, the cattle prod jolting him with enough electricity to take down something twice his size. Even a guy with his strength and enhancements couldn't hold up against that.

Dallas momentarily thought how nice it might be if Rita were a wolf or a bear shifter. Hell, he'd even take a big cat. Anything that would be useful in a fight.

Even if she'd switched to her raccoon form, there wouldn't be much she could do to help him in this fight.

Luckily, Rita had figured that out already, because he heard her voice from a distance. "Yes, 911?" Rita gave their location, but as she did, two of the guards started moving in her direction.

Dallas grabbed onto their legs, holding them back. He wished the electrical current would run through him and into them, but that wasn't the case. Instead, he held on tight, summoning any last bit of strength he had to keep them away from Rita.

"Let go!" Bryce shouted, pulling the prod out and hitting Dallas in the head, as though that would make him release the other men.

"Then don't go after her." Dallas grit his teeth, feeling sweat on his forehead. He wouldn't be able to hold out much longer. In the minutes it might take the closest patrol car to arrive, Lilly's guards could get both of them into the nondescript black van that had its doors open, waiting for them.

All three men had turned their attention away from Rita and were trying to pry Dallas' hands off. Dallas still fought as best as he could, but the swings of his fists were sloppy at best.

As Bryce was trying to get a metal cord around Dallas'

wrist, he saw Rita come up behind him. He'd tucked the cattle prod away, and without hesitation, she pulled it out and jabbed it into Bryce's stomach.

With an "oof," Bryce dropped the cord but then looked at Rita with his brows raised.

She hadn't turned it on.

"Give me—"

Dallas watched Rita turn on the cattle prod, and Bryce screamed long and loud, falling to his side and curling up. They didn't have a chance to celebrate the small victory as the other two men, who Dallas was holding on to, turned their attention to her.

She was within their reach, and one managed to grab her and hook one of the metal cords to her arm. "What is this?" She shrieked. "I can't shift out of it!"

He watched her as she struggled but failed to free herself. He felt his heart sink. It was over. They had her.

"Help! Someone help!" Her cry for help wasn't nearly loud enough to alert anyone. The current in the wire was subduing her.

Even so, there had to be someone in her building. Someone who would hear the commotion and come out to see what the fuss was about before the police got there.

No one was coming. Dallas had to do it. He pulled all the strength he could, the effects of the cattle prod still hampering his efforts. He managed to pull the guards' legs out from under them. They went down, struggling, but Dallas managed to crawl forward, grabbing their belts, then their shirts, until finally, his massive hands held both of their heads.

With a loud "crack," he smacked them together hard and fast.

Their sunglasses either broke, or the shades fell right off

their faces as both men melted down and fell onto the hot asphalt of the parking lot.

"Breathe," Dallas croaked, reaching Rita. "You have to calm down." He reached a hand out, placing it over her heart, feeling it racing.

He breathed in a deep breath, hoping she would mimic him.

She did. Then she mimicked his breath out. He offered her his metal hand, and she took it immediately. He pulled her up to her feet as though she weighed nothing at all.

"I'm glad you're okay," she said, her face full of worry.

He scowled, assessing all the blood on her. "You're bleeding."

"What?"

He indicated her shoulder. She looked, finally seeing the blood oozing through her shirt.

"Fuck. The stitches probably tore, and I didn't even feel it."

"Thanks to all the adrenaline. Are you okay?"

"Yes, how about you?"

A voice called out from the apartment building. "Are you all right down there?"

They looked up towards the window. Someone had seen them. An old man leaned out his window and stared at both of them with concern in his eyes.

"We're fine, thank you."

"Do you want me to call the police?"

"They're already coming, don't worry," Rita said, but then added, "But maybe it won't hurt to call them again just in case?"

The old man in the window nodded. He looked at Dallas funny, but then ducked his head back into his apartment and shut the window.

"He's probably wondering if I'm one of your attackers."

"So long as he calls the police, I don't care.."

"Dallas..."

They stopped and looked back quickly. Bryce was on one knee. His arm wrapped around his middle. He was sweating, his sunglasses off.

He looked like a normal guy without the shades on.

"You know she's not going to stop. She won't stop."

"That's fine. I won't stop either. You go back, and you tell that bitch that I'm going to get her back for doing this to me."

Bryce smiled. "Right, if she doesn't drink me dry first."

"Then tell it to her politely. Either way, I hope she got her fill of me because she's going to be real sick of me, soon."

Dallas approached Bryce, who stayed on one knee. He held out his hand, but it wasn't in a show of peace or friendship. "Give me the key to the van."

Bryce shut his eyes. He looked down at the asphalt. He looked almost as tired as Dallas, but then he nodded. "Whatever. Can't get much worse than this."

He reached into his pocket. Rita tensed, but Dallas stayed calm, and Bryce didn't try any other dirty tricks.

He pulled out the keys and handed them over.

Dallas looked at them, then away at the sound of sirens howling in the sky.

He looked back at Rita. "We need to go."

"No kidding." Rita pointed a finger at Bryce, in a pose that looked like she was trying to be as threatening as possible. "If you or any of your friends get into my apartment again and mess around with my stuff, there's gonna be hell to pay."

"Don't worry, we weren't pilfering your underwear drawer," Bryce deadpanned.

It really looked like everyone had stopped giving a shit.

They were clearly over it, and maybe Bryce would get away. He was still awake, but his two friends were done.

Rita and Dallas climbed into the van. Dallas started the engine, and they began driving, taking the second entrance to the parking lot so they wouldn't get stopped by the police.

As the sounds of sirens got farther and farther away, Dallas craned his neck to see what was in the back seat of the van.

There was a gurney back there. A few medical supplies and an IV drip. Weapons were mounted to the walls of the van, and a long black box undoubtedly filled with horrors.

Rita looked back too. "Woah, it looks like a torture chamber back there."

They'd likely been planning on putting Dallas back into a coma and presenting him to Lilly like ants would to their queen.

"Okay, you really need to tell me what's going on now."

"That's not any of your business."

"Screw you, it's not. I just got held down by two guys and chased away from my apartment. I'm the one who keeps getting injured here. Why does Lilly want you so much? Why did she do this to you?"

Dallas pressed his lips together. Then he punched the steering wheel.

Rita jumped. He'd done that with his metal hand, and now there was definitely a noticeable dent in the wheel.

"Fuck," Dallas cursed again and again at himself for damaging their ride, and at her for putting him into this position.

"I should drop you off at a shelter," he said.

Rita was aghast. "Don't you even think about it."

"It's safer for you to be away from me."

"I brought you to where I live, and they saw my face. I'm going with you, you're telling me what's going on, and then we're dealing with this shit together."

"Uh-huh." He stared ahead, but then the corner of his mouth quirked up in a smile. "You're really going to stick this out with me, aren't you?"

"Well, I did you such a huge favor by breaking you out of that place. Then all this happens. Yeah, I'm sticking with you to make sure you don't get dragged back to that vault."

Finally, Dallas seemed to come to a decision. "All right, then I need to let you know something. I'm not entirely human. Or even entirely human-cyborg."

Rita laughed and rolled her eyes. "Why do you say it like you're going to say something that shocks me? I can't smell shifter on you, so unless you're going to say something like Lilly wants your blood because you're a fairy or something—"

"Actually, that's exactly it."

NINE

Rita had been so close to telling Dallas her secrets.

They said the matchmaker was never wrong. That she had a track record of finding someone's perfect match. People came to her from far and wide to find who the loves of their lives would be.

If that much was true for her and Dallas, then she couldn't exactly walk away from him now.

She had to keep her potential match out of Lilly's grasp. He would be of no use to her—or her future plans—locked up and sucked dry.

But then he'd gone and changed things.

Shit.

Rita tensed. She hadn't expected that.

"Are you serious?"

He smiled. "I know, such a stereotype, right?"

"Uh, yeah, no kidding."

Vampires were supposed to love how fairy blood tasted. There was a rumor that drinking it was not only delicious for them but that it would allow them to walk around during the daylight.

Which was, of course, proven nonsense.

No vampire could ever walk under the sun without there being dire consequences for them. Everyone knew that.

But some vampires still loved a good pint of fairy blood. Some fairies even sold their blood to vampires for a pretty penny.

Rita knew this because she'd stolen from the occasional fairy and seen what was hidden within their safes.

None of this clarified their situation.

"If you're a fairy, then why would she bother with locking you up? Why is your arm missing? Why not just buy some pre-bottle blood?"

Dallas checked the rearview mirror, as though searching for anyone who could be tailing them.

Or the police.

"She can buy all the fairy blood she likes. Get the purest stuff on the market and drink it every day if she wants. But she was using me for a different reason."

His metal fingers tapped the dented steering wheel.

"I think in the past, she's had issues with hosts. It takes a long time to recover from a blood donation, and sometimes drain sites get infected. She wanted to create something that would produce faster, heal better, and also be compliant for the long-term."

Suddenly, Rita was upset with herself for asking him these questions. Lilly was trying to make him into a fairy-blood factory?

"I'm sorry. I shouldn't have asked. If it's too much, I'll shut up now."

"No, it's okay. You're right. You saved me, and I should tell you what you walked in there for. If this... witch matched you with me, then I guess you have more of a vested interest in this than what's just on the surface."

Rita almost didn't catch that. "Wait. What? I thought you didn't know who she was?"

"I couldn't remember at the time you asked. I don't personally know any witches who specialize in soul mates or love. It came back to me when I saw her card in your bag at the hospital. The hearts looked familiar."

Rita sat back, stunned. Why hadn't he said anything?

He shook his head. "I have no idea how I got on her list. Maybe one of the other guys put me on as a joke. Bill was a prick, but he was always saying I needed to get laid. But I figured, if she sent you to me, it was for a reason."

He looked pointedly at her. There was nothing disappointed in his blue eyes. "We're mates, aren't we?"

It didn't sound like much of a question.

Rita was so humiliated. "So you found out what I'm... well, wait, just because I busted you out doesn't mean that's what was going on. I didn't necessarily free you to get her services. You could easily be for someone else."

She didn't want him to know she'd felt desperate enough to go to a matchmaking witch. That was too much. She couldn't be that pathetic to him.

His smile looked so...soft. Nothing cruel, nothing to suggest he was making fun of her.

Even the metal plating on his face couldn't take away from it. "I thought so at first, but the way you just said that tells me otherwise."

"It does?" Rita squeaked.

"You're a professional thief, and you busted me out of that place. I'm clearly who you were matched up with."

She was going to die. She was actually going to vanish from her seat and die.

"I'm not a... I mean, I don't always..."

"Why are you embarrassed?"

She didn't want to face him. "I don't know. I don't know why this is suddenly so embarrassing. It shouldn't be. I don't think. I only take from people who can afford it."

"Which is still stealing."

"But I make sure they deserve it."

"Which is subjective to you," Dallas said. "But if you're asking me to judge you for it, I can't exactly do that either, not considering who I worked for."

He took a deep breath. "I wouldn't have gotten out of there if you hadn't woken me up, either."

"I didn't wake you up." Rita was salty about this whole thing now. The fact that he'd known this entire time and he hadn't told her? She didn't know how she was supposed to feel about that.

"Yes, you did."

"No, I didn't." She might as well be as honest as she could be about this one thing. They'd lied to each other and kept things from each other since they first met. She didn't want him to think she was some sort of savior to him either. "I walked into that room where you were being kept, and you woke up on your own. Maybe whatever it was they were using to keep you knocked out wore off or ran out." She said, remembering the tubes that had been plugged into his body.

"You would have gotten up on your own, found a way to get out of that gurney with that stupid strength you have, and broke out on your own eventually."

"I woke up for a reason."

"I know. I just said that."

"No, I'm saying that I woke up because of you."

She looked at him, frowning. "What?"

He didn't take his eyes off the road, responsible driver that he was. "I smelled something in the room with me. Something good. I knew I had to see it. It... pulled me awake. I had to see you."

He glanced at her, but only briefly. "I needed to see you. Your smell woke me up, and then you let me out. Then I found out you were smart enough to get some of those double locks picked." Dallas shook his head. "There was no way I was getting out of there without help. I don't know who gave my name to your matchmaker, but I'm glad they did it because it brought me you."

Rita's chest felt all fluttery and weird. She couldn't quite put her finger on it, but it was there.

"Um, maybe one of your friends gave out your name after you were locked up? She clearly knew you were going to be in that vault."

She was supposed to be a bit firecracker of a woman, hard to read, and always surprising people, but Rita didn't know much else about her aside from that.

"Unless she's also a psychic...I don't know. It is possible. Nothing is impossible in this scenario."

"Maybe it was Bryce? Or you said there was someone named Bill? They could have used it as a way to call for help for you."

Dallas got quiet at the suggestion. Rita suddenly wasn't so sure it was a good idea to give it. To give him some hope that maybe his friends were still trying to look out for him after helping to lock him up.

Hell, he could have easily given his own name one night when he was too drunk to remember it. His friends might not have had anything to do with it.

When Dallas did speak, his voice was somber. "If they did have anything to do with it, then do me a favor and don't repeat it. I don't want to take the risk that Lilly ever suspects something like this. Better that it just be a coincidence."

"We can go and ask her right now."

"No. I'm not doing that either," Dallas said. "I want you to have plausible deniability, and I want the same for me. If anything ever happens to either of us, I don't want Lilly to think someone in her house is working against her." Dallas clenched his fists.

"Even if they don't deserve it."

Right. It would be a while before he could forgive the other men he'd worked with.

"You don't want to take the risk that they just left you to rot, do you?"

Dallas shook his head. "I don't want to stab someone in the back like that. Not even to save myself."

Rita tensed. "I...that wasn't what I meant. I just..."

"I know," Dallas said. He briefly looked away from the road again, but he didn't hold eye contact with her for long. "I know what you meant. Don't worry. You don't seem like the type who would be into doing that to someone else. Not after breaking me out of that prison."

"But...how do you know I wouldn't have left you behind? When I was in the window, I thought about jumping and leaving you."

"But you didn't."

"Because I got shot."

"Which means you and I don't know if you would have jumped, so don't judge yourself as though you had."

Her heart swelled in that moment.

He was offering her an olive branch, and screw it; she was taking it.

Rita believed he wasn't just letting her off the hook. He

was accepting that she wasn't going to be that sort of person.

Rita couldn't stand people like that. She couldn't believe she'd said something that gave him the impression, even for a second, that she was like that.

"So, where are we going?"

Dallas breathed deep through his nose. "To be honest, right now? I don't know. Just away from here. We can wait for the police to be finished with what they're doing. When they leave, we can go back and get some of your things."

"We could try to find the matchmaker," Rita suggested. "She doesn't exactly open up the invitations, but when she knows people want to find her, she lets herself be found."

Dallas raised a brow at her. "That doesn't sound promising."

"I mean, no," Rita said. "And it wouldn't be to ask her about where your name came from, but she knows people. Maybe we can find someone to help lead us to her."

Dallas seemed to think about it. "This is your suggestion?"

"I'd really rather not do this alone. She seems like she's hanging around with good people. I think they would help us if we asked."

Dallas pressed his lips together. "All right then."

Rita blinked. She'd expected more of a fight than that. "Really?"

"Yes," he nodded. "Really. You've at least met these people, and if you're right, then she had something to do with getting me out of there. Even if one of my old buddies didn't give her my name, then she's still responsible for getting me out of there as much as you are."

"More so, probably."

"She's not the one who did all the physical work. No offense to the woman."

Rita smiled. "I won't tell her you said that."

"But... to be honest, there is something we need to do before going to see her."

"Really? What's that?"

He hesitated before responding.

Rita's stomach swirled with anticipation. He knew they were being paired together by *the* matchmaker extraordinaire. There was only one possible thing he could want, right? Rita was shockingly eager to hear him come out and say it.

"We need to take a look at your stitches."

Rita deflated.

That... was definitely not what she'd expected him to say.

CHAPTER

TEN

They waited for three hours. Driving around in a stolen van wasn't the best idea in the world, so they dumped it two miles away from her apartment and walked back.

The police were long gone by the time they made it back, which was a plus, as Rita was not in the mood to do any more lying or explaining.

"I'm sorry," Dallas said suddenly. "I should be taking care of some of this for you, not dumping it all off on you."

He looked wrecked. Ashamed. Irritated they had to do this at all.

Rita didn't want that for him.

She shrugged, making no big deal of it. "I'm a thief, right? We have to throw everything away and start fresh every couple of years anyway. I mean, if we don't want to get caught."

"Makes sense," Dallas said. "I still want to take a look at your stitches before we get out of here. Do you have a first aid kit?"

"Under the bathroom sink."

Rita realized it might be a good idea to take that with her when they left here.

She normally had her list of important items memorized and ready to go in her head for just such an emergency as this.

But she was frazzled. Too much had happened too soon.

She was starting over. She was going to have to get a whole new name, go to a new town, and start from scratch.

But, for the first time in her life, she would be doing all that while someone was there to share it with her.

Which was kind of the point of going to the matchmaker in the first place.

It wasn't just being a shifter that complicated her dating life. It was her line of work, but now that Dallas knew what she was, had admitted to knowing, and didn't judge her for it, Rita felt alive and hopeful in a way she had never before experienced.

If she wanted to go straight, she could do that with Dallas beside her. Not because it was something she had to do or because she needed to hide her past from the person she fell in love with.

No. It would be because she was choosing to do it.

And that made her feel all kinds of optimistic. Even though there had been uninvited guests in her apartment only a few hours ago, and her shoulder was killing her, Rita was actually in one of the better moods of her life.

The fact that Dallas could see all the dirty dishes in her sink didn't bother her a bit.

And, miracle of miracles, Bryce had been telling the truth when he'd admitted to not having gone through her underwear drawers.

It looked exactly as she had left it. Panties still kind of messy, but definitely untouched by anyone but her.

Packing some of her sexy panties seemed like a good idea if she was going to be on the road with Dallas.

That warm feeling flooded her chest and neck again as she packed them away.

If he was her match, her true mate, then he would soon see her wearing them.

God, she'd never cared about how nice she'd looked in her underwear, and here she was, wondering if a guy who had metal plates on his face and arm would find any faults in her body.

She shook her head. He wouldn't. If he did, then he wouldn't be a proper match, would he?

"All right, first aid kit," Dallas said, coming into her room, jolting her out of her sexy thoughts.

She shoved her panties into the deepest part of her pack, clearing her throat. "Right. Okay."

"Take a seat."

She did as she was told, feeling oddly more mechanical than Dallas. "We don't have long, do we?"

He shook his head, opening the case. "Not really. Lilly is going to realize Bryce failed even before he can give his report. We need to be out of here before then. Open your shirt."

She did. Rita couldn't help but smile as she did so, quickly, but not *too* quickly, exposing herself for him.

Dallas shook his head at her, as though he could read her mind. "Don't even think about it. That's not what I'm thinking about it, and we don't have time for it anyway."

"Right, right. We just have a few minutes for me to pack my things and for you to take a look at my shoulder."

He nodded. "Exactly."

He was either being purposely dense, or he really couldn't read that she was trying to flirt with him.

He'd figured out a lot on his own, and so Rita was willing to bet that he was intentionally ignoring her advances.

Dallas' fingers were quick as he checked her stitches. He was calm as he worked, which helped.

"Does it hurt?"

"Both physically and my pride," she said. "I think the thing that annoys me the most is that these stitches were fresh."

Dallas didn't say anything to her for a little while. He cleaned the wound, pulled the stitches out, and sewed her back up. He seemed to be trying to put the needle through the holes that had already been made in her, which she definitely appreciated.

"So, a fairy, eh?"

He shook his head, the corner of his lips, quirking. "Quarter fairy. Barely amounts to anything."

"You didn't have wings or anything, did you?"

She was genuinely curious about that.

He laughed. "No, nothing like that, so you don't have to worry."

She was glad. Having wings would have been fascinating, but the fact that he didn't have any now...She would rather he never had them at all, than for him to have once had them, just for some vampire bitch to take them away.

Rita flinched at the cold touch of his metal fingers, so close to her tender wound.

"Sorry."

"S'Okay," she said, heart thudding.

The fact that his metal hand seemed to do such a good and steady job of giving her new stitches made her think.

"Why did she give you new limbs? If she hated you that much—"

"Lilly doesn't hate me," Dallas said. A little too quickly.

Now Rita was the one to figure things out. "Was she in love with you?"

Dallas finished, and he snipped away the extra thread before he replied.

"Yes. For whatever that would mean for her."

Rita couldn't believe it. "Really?"

He stared hard at her.

Rita flushed. "I mean, not that you're not worth it. You're definitely good-looking."

Super good-looking. Rita didn't blame his boss for having the hots for him.

"I don't think it was entirely to do with my looks," he said, scratching at the back of his neck. "I think it was more to do with my fae blood."

Rita didn't get it. "What's that got to do with anything?"

"Vampires like it, apparently," he said. "But I'm not a full blood, or even half. I didn't see the appeal, or believe she would take any benefits from it regardless of whether or not I gave her any."

Rita shivered. "So, she locked you up to get your blood?"

"I think it was more to do with her being unused to not getting what she wants. When I turned her down, she decided she was going to keep me around and drink my blood anyway."

He clenched his teeth and fists, looking downright mean, nasty, and utterly furious for the first time since she'd met him. "I was an idiot for thinking she wouldn't go this far. I knew better. I knew *her*. I thought I did."

Rita flinched. "God, I'm...so sorry."

Dallas's shoulders vibrated with that pent-up anger,

that energy. Rita felt his fury and his helplessness for trusting a woman who went around the law.

Like Rita did.

Then he exhaled, like a volcano releasing smoke and steam instead of a more horrible eruption.

He plopped next to her on her bed, his elbows on his knees, hands threading through his hair. "If you're worried that I see her when I look at you, no. Definitely not. You and she are polar opposites. I mean, Lilly stole things plenty of times, but her idea of who deserved it and who didn't was different from yours."

She smiled at that, secretly relieved. "You keep complimenting me like that, and I'm going to start getting ideas."

"I haven't said anything about you that wasn't true."

That was exactly why she felt complimented.

He looked right at her, and Rita froze, realizing she was staring at him.

Neither of them looked away from the other. That heady, heart-thumping feeling came back to her, and when Dallas' eyes glanced down at her mouth, she knew what he wanted.

"You saved my life," he said. "I won't let anything happen to you."

"I think you need someone to watch out for you just as much," she joked.

Dallas shook his head, but then he reached for her, his metal hand finding the back of her neck.

She didn't fight him as he pulled her closer, kissing her on the mouth. He had a rough stubble around his lips and jaw. She liked that. A scratchy jaw got to her every time.

Christ, he just had to be perfect for her in every way, didn't he?

Rita grabbed his arm, just for something to hold onto.

The cold metal of his forearm was a stark contrast in comparison to the heat and softness of his mouth. He pulled her close, and she straddled his lap, fitting on him perfectly as she rubbed against him.

"Do you think she'll send people right away?" Rita whispered. "Or do you think there's a chance they'll take a day to regroup?"

Because no matter what happened, the one thing they could count on was that Lilly *would* be coming. They were free and clear tonight, but she was still out there.

They would be dealing with this whole thing, with her, for a while.

Dallas groaned, "I'm willing to take the risk."

Rita smiled, pulling her shirt the rest of the way off and tugging at his. She was starting to realize that he might just be as much of an adrenaline junkie as she was.

Their breath quickened, and their hands explored each other's bodies while they shed their clothes. Dallas was careful to avoid her shoulder, except for the light kisses he left there.

With not a lot of time, and knowing anyone could bust in on them at any moment, they wasted no seconds. Rita stared into his eyes as she lowered herself onto him, taking in his thickness and enjoying each inch.

When he filled her to the hilt, she shuddered and let out a moan of pleasure. "You feel so good. Just perfect."

"Are you going to do it?" He asked.

In response, she started to move her hips. He met her rhythm. "Like this?" She asked.

"No, I mean, yes, this is fucking great, don't stop, but I meant the mark. Don't you have to mark me, so we can make this thing official?"

She stared into his green eyes as she rode him, taking

a moment to process what he was saying. "You barely know me. Don't you want us to get to know each other first?"

He shook his head before dipping his head to kiss her neck. His hands traced her hips and her waist and went up until he held both of her breasts in his hands. He traced her nipples with his fingers, heightening all the sensations in her body. "I don't have a single doubt about us. It feels right, and we have the blessing of the best matchmaker in the paranormal world, right?"

Rita nodded, feeling her body start to tense. "I'm close." She told him, shocked at how quick it was happening. She didn't know if it was the attraction she had to him, the fact that it had been a while since her last lay, or maybe some magic of their mating, but she was ready to go over the edge with him.

"Me too," Dallas said, starting to buck even harder.

Rita readied herself, placing her teeth on his skin-covered shoulder. She started to kiss, then suck at the flesh, and as their bodies reached their orgasms together, Rita bit down, leaving her mark on her mate.

She felt Dallas do the same on her opposite shoulder—the uninjured one. Fairies didn't need to mark their mate, but she liked it all the same. It was something her kind did, and she would love having it on her as a permanent symbol of their lasting connection.

Rita's body pulsed, and both of their thrusts turned into more of a rocking until finally, they stilled, and Rita collapsed on top of him. They breathed in unison, feeling the echoes of their orgasms fade and leave a heart connection in their wake.

This is love. Rita thought, knowing without a doubt that it was true.

When she finally pulled back, Rita blinked a little, trying to clear her head, but she was smiling.

"What?" He asked.

She chuckled. "I think this was just a preview of what we're going to do to each other." Rita slapped his knee. "Now, let's get on the road and on the way to making a new life."

The End

... actually, just the beginning!

Rita and Dallas are back in each of the following stories in this series... you see, Esme the matchmaker has a sister named Harmony who feels like all won't be right in the raccoon's world until she's reunited with her triplet sisters!

They have a lot more to do before they finally face off with Lilly in Book 5!

SHAPE UP OR SHIFT OUT SERIES

A Rose by Any Other Name
Winter of Discontent
Sea of Trouble
The Better Part of Valor
Etched in Brass

About the Author

USA Today Bestselling Author Mandy Rosko is a videogame playing, book loving chick. She loves writing paranormal romances that range from light steamy to erotic, and has some contemporary and historical romances as well. You can find her on all sorts of platforms, including Twitch, where she does writing sprints, crafting, and video gaming!

Get all the latest news from Mandy by signing up for her newsletter: subscribepage.com/mandyroskobooks

As a bonus for signing up, you'll get her starter library, including Burns Like Fire, Sold to the Enemy, and The Vampire's Curse!

facebook.com/MandyRoskoRomance

instagram.com/mandyroskodraws

amazon.com/Mandy-Rosko/e/B008ETBVFW

bookbub.com/authors/mandy-rosko

goodreads.com/mandyrosko

youtube.com/UCD1z6r06dKoN-0WdUbi1pAQ

ALSO BY MANDY ROSKO

PARANORMAL ROMANCE

Blood Secrets

Darkness Awakened

Passion Awakened

Beauty Awakened (Coming Soon)

Eve Langlais' FUCN'A

I'll Be Dammed

Trash Queen

Chillin' Out

Bits and Bobs

Poisoned Kisses

Goddesses of Vengeance

Angel's Fury

Shape Up or Shift Out

A Rose by Any Other Name

Winter of Discontent

Sea of Trouble

The Better Part of Valor

Etched in Brass (Coming Soon)

Shifter Hospital

Alpha Medicine

Second Chance Alpha (Coming Soon)

The Aquaterrestrial Task Force

Get Kraken

Shark Bait

The Nightshade Guild

Mage to Disobey

Magic Confined

Defying Time

Crimson Moon Hideaway

(Amazon and KU Only)

Double Booked with Her Ex

Flame and Mist

Learn more at mandyrosko.com

www.ingramcontent.com/pod-product-compliance
Lightning Source LLC
Chambersburg PA
CBHW052141150726

48002CB00003B/1020